W9-AXA-485

SCOTT COUNTY LIBRARY
SHAKOPEE, MN 55379

World of Reading

STAR WARS

ESCAPE FROM DARTH VADER

WRITTEN BY MICHAEL SIGLAIN

ART BY STEPHANE ROUX

Los Angeles • New York

ABDOPUBLISHING.COM

Reinforced library bound edition published in 2016 by Spotlight, a division of ABDO
PO Box 398166, Minneapolis, Minnesota 55439. Spotlight produces high-quality
reinforced library bound editions for schools and libraries. Published by
Disney • Lucasfilm Press, an imprint of Disney Book Group.

Printed in the United States of America, North Mankato, Minnesota.
042015
092015

Copyright © 2014 Lucasfilm Ltd. & ® or TM. All rights reserved. Published by
Disney • Lucasfilm Press, an imprint of Disney Book Group. No part of this book may
be reproduced or transmitted in any form or by any means, electronic or mechanical,
including photocopying, recording, or by any information storage and retrieval
system, without written permission from the publisher. For information address
Disney • Lucasfilm Press, 1101 Flower Street, Glendale, California 91201.

LIBRARY OF CONGRESS CATALOGING-IN-PUBLICATION DATA

This title was previously cataloged with the following information:

Siglain, Michael.
Star Wars : Escape from Darth Vader / by Michael Siglain ; illustrated by Stephane Roux.
p. cm. (World of reading ; Level 1)
Summary: Trying to keep the Rebel's secret plans from Darth Vader, robots C-3PO and R2D2 crash land on Tatooine and meet a young farmer named Luke.
1. Extraterrestrial beings--Juvenile fiction. 2. Robots--Juvenile fiction. 3. Humorous stories. I. Roux, Stephane, ill.
[E]--dc23
PZ7.G5624 Ho 2014
2014937083

978-1-61479-364-9 (reinforced library bound edition)

Spotlight
A Division of ABDO
abdopublishing.com

Long ago
and far, far away . . .

a small ship
was under attack.

It was being chased
by a big ship.

Inside the small ship
were two droids.

One droid was short,
and the other was tall.

The tall droid
was named C-3PO.

He was worried.
He thought they
were doomed.

The short droid
was named R2-D2.

He was not worried.
He wanted to find
the princess.

The princess
was named Leia.

Princess Leia had
secret battle plans.

The troopers
from the big ship

wanted to steal the
secret battle plans.

The troopers
ran through
the small ship.

Then Darth Vader appeared.

Darth Vader
was a Sith Lord.
He was mean and scary.

Darth Vader ordered the troopers to search the ship.

Princess Leia had to
keep the secret plans
hidden from Darth Vader.

She gave them to R2-D2
to keep them safe.

Then Princess Leia
hid from
Darth Vader.

But the troopers
were still looking
for the princess.

Princess Leia attacked the troopers.

But the troopers
captured her.
They brought her to
Darth Vader.

The princess did not
tell Darth Vader
that R2-D2 had the plans.

No one knew where
R2-D2 was.
Then C-3PO found him.

R2-D2 got inside an escape pod.

He had to get the plans off the ship.

C-3PO followed R2-D2 into the pod.

The pod flew away from the big ship.

The droids escaped
from Darth Vader!

They landed on a
very sandy planet.

Now a new journey
was about to begin
for R2-D2 and C-3PO!